For P. Jr. and his thousand-yard stare.
Thanks Ben, Bree, and Dean (Black Hare Press) for your interest!

x
Paul, July 2020

HADES II

PAUL WARMERDAM

Available from Black Hare Press in 2020

SHORT READS

WARDENCLYFFE by GREGG CUNNINGHAM
HADES 11 by PAUL WARMERDAM
BLOOD AND SILK by ZOEY XOLTON
AS ABOVE, SO BENEATH by JOSHUA D. TAYLOR
DEAD MAN WALKING by DAVID GREEN
THE RISE OF THE GREAT OLD ONE by JASMINE JARVIS
YAWRISOD AND THE ABOMINATION by SHAWN M. KLIMEK

UNDERGROUND

MIRACLE GROWTH by TIM MENDEES
THE RETURN by GABRIELLA BALCOM
UNDERGROUND by S. GEPP
WHISPERS IN THE DARK by K.B. ELIJAH
SWIRLING DARKNESS by SAM M. PHILLIPS
THE GATE TO THE UNDERWORLD by E.L. GILES
COLD AS HELL by NEEN COHEN

Twitter: @BlackHarePress
Facebook: BlackHarePress
Website: www.BlackHarePress.com

Over six million pounds of thrust would soon separate Dirk and Kris from the Earth that had given birth to them and three and a half billion others. They weren't doing it for the others. The Hades program was proving that humanity could be forsaken.

All of history had led to these missions—every war and every advancement in technology. It has not been two decades since the first nuclear attack of one nation against another. Once one war was over, the tensions for the next were already fostered between its victors. Years of fear followed, with ever-mounting tensions—an arms race on rocket fuel. There was a day everyone could see looming ahead of them, a day everyone dreaded. When it came, it was sooner than they had wished. Nothing had been the same since.

The astronauts shared a look. A countdown was started in the firing room as their pale and glazing eyes met. This was the launch of their program's eleventh flight. Kris looked almost like a child in the bulk of her spacesuit. Her once sweet face held a rictus of anticipation. By contrast, Dirk's seat could barely contain his broad frame. He ground his rotting teeth, thinking about the atrocities that had brought them to this moment.

There had been protests—the living did not want to see the part they had played in their history. They did not understand the Hades missions, and so they resisted them. The dead had proved they were not easily pacified—their global nation had asserted that nothing would stop these missions. Nothing the living tried could change that.

Dirk performed the very last checks. Kris nodded in agreement. Nothing stood in their way now. Launch control confirmed it. The pad shook. The water deluge came and went. The entire tower rumbled.

It was said that the Resurrection Event had been more than mere mercy. Even if it were some kind of redemption, there had been no reprieve from the persecution that followed. There were those, like Dirk, who would not have stopped after the liberation. With the formation of the Nation of the Dead, there were also those, like Kris, who aspired to something else. It was not a human pursuit that was able to unite them in the end. It was something more, something new. In this dream they began to share, the dead would go beyond the reach of the living, and the living would be spared, granted the chance to change, allowed to continue, but never absolved.

One voice after the next added its confirmation: "Go for launch." The world was watching a live broadcast in horror. Dirk imagined all those war criminals shuddering at their pails. Today, the dead would forsake the living and prove that they could transcend what was done to them.

The dream not only gave the dead something to build on after the living were overthrown, but it also mitigated the unyielding wrath among them. Dirk was one of those who couldn't forgive the living. If it hadn't been for voices like Kris', there would have been executions instead of incarcerations. Dirk wouldn't have been where he was.

They had passed the three-minute mark. The sequence was entirely automated beyond this point. Their fate was in the hands of a computer in the firing room. Messages were being passed along to the astronauts. Among them were words of apology and wishes for their fortune. Dirk transmitted a curt response: "Tell them we already know it will be a good flight."

The living had been powerless to stop the previous missions, just as they were powerless to stop this one. They watched as their own tools of war were reshaped into a new purpose, working toward the dream they couldn't share. The dead would put the first man and woman on the moon, and it would only be their first step. Nothing would stand in their way.

The countdown reached its last seconds without any failures. Dirk looked up at Kris one more time. All engines were running; the noise was incredible. The commit signal passed. Kris smiled once before they were thrust from Earth. The same force of violence that had once propelled decimation was now harnessed to liberate those it had claimed.

The blast stirred more memories in Dirk. He remembered the fire in the sky and how the shockwaves had ripped through the ground. In the confined space aboard the Hades 11, he relived the death that had come for him years ago. It had been the day everyone had dreaded. The next morning, no one had any explanation—the bombs had produced corpses when there should have been nothing left but dust. Some said the Resurrection Event was a cruel trick of physics. Others said it was an act of compassion on the part of the scientists charged with designing the atomic weapons. When the leaders of the living came out of their shelters, they watched the corpses rise, watched the soldiers forsake the lives these wars had made for them, and finally watched as the old structures crumbled and their power dissolved. After years of mounting tension, after their escalation of nuclear threats, the fate of the world was no longer in their hands.

Their rocket was still picking up speed. Dirk made contact with the tracking stations spread all over the globe. Kris informed him that they were starting to level off. First and second rocket stages had come and gone, leaving their husks empty of fuel to plummet back down to Earth. They had been brought into orbit.

To this day, the Resurrection Event has been debated. A certain degree of mysticism surrounded the scientists who had designed the weapons. Before there was a chance for them to address the Nation of the Dead, they had disappeared, never to be seen again. Dirk believed what most of his kind believed; they had disappeared while the leaders of the living still wielded some of the power they had fostered. They must have felt the instincts of exposed vermin. They must have acted without hesitation. They must have gotten to the scientists first. It was the one thing he feared now—that the living had learned something about the dead that they had yet to discover for themselves.

Outside, Earth's surface rolled back, showing its distinct continents. Not one of them had been spared the scars of atomic warfare, the pinnacle of the civilisation of the living. Dirk's rasping voice broke a long silence, "To put such deeds behind you is a trial for the cold-blooded."

Kris did not look back. Her eyes were fixed on the darkness ahead of them. Dirk could not bring up his fears. He shared a long history with Kris, but even with her, he did not dare give voice to the notion that some atrocities still lay ahead of them.

When twelve minutes had passed since the launch, they finally ceased to accelerate. "These were not…the first," Kris answered in her pained and halting manner, "injustices…in the world." Death had left its marks on all of them. For Kris, it had left her straining with the effort to speak. "Maybe one day…we'll look back and…see that Earth was…a crucible." Kris winced. "From its fires…we alone…will have cast…ourselves into a…mould of our own…choosing."

Dirk narrowed his eyes and looked outside again. Earth turned below them, exposed. All of history had played out down there. Now, on the 16th of July 1969, came the future.

In the vast gyration of Earth's orbit, the Hades 11 waited. As the launch site back on Earth was cleared of ambassadors and news agencies, Dirk and Kris prepared to leave Earth's grip at precisely the right time. Coverage of their journey was still being broadcast all over the globe below them.

"Our…transcendence…has   its…witnesses," Kris said, amused.

"Let them see all of it. Sooner or later, the

message has to sink in."

"What…message…is that?"

"That they have lost. That they will be left behind, all of them. Transcendence, like you said."

Kris looked away. Each hour that passed by brought her closer to her most critical role on board. She was the command module's pilot, in charge of the manoeuvres that would get them into the moon's orbit. Dirk would take the lead for the most crucial part of the mission, but not before she brought them to that point.

They had completed one and a half orbits when it was time. Kris burned the third stage's trans-lunar injection and performed the procedures to retrieve and attach the lunar module. After transposition, extraction, and docking, they were turned around, facing away from Earth. They were finally putting it behind them. Every hour passing now was an hour closer to their destination. It was a three-day journey in total, covering a distance of more than two hundred thousand miles, to the moon.

Messages exchanged with Earth remained frequent. They marked a trajectory that would allow their final stage rockets to slingshot around their destination and enter the sun's orbit, leaving Dirk and Kris to enter the moon's.

Kris was waiting for the moment when the Earth and the moon appeared the same size from where they could see. It was their second day in transit when Dirk tried repeating himself in a transmission to mission control. For the first time, there had been no response. He repeated himself a third time.

"Be…patient," Kris said. "They…have whole…teams of…engineers…who…must have…noticed…the same."

Dirk shrugged irritably. He motioned to transmit a fourth time, then changed his mind.

"Don't…worry." Kris motioned for Dirk to join him. He knew she was only trying to distract him as she pointed out the small triangular window. He humoured her and watched the moon expand ever so slowly ahead of them.

It wasn't until two hours later that they received a message from mission control. Dirk immediately insisted on an explanation. Their messages were clear and uninterrupted now. Mission control only said that their equipment had malfunctioned. Kris saw the look on Dirk's face and responded before he had the chance.

"Tell…us…everything. We…don't want…to be…distracted…by wondering."

"The equipment was interfered with," mission control admitted at last, then followed up with three short messages.

"It's fine now."

"There's no need to worry."

"Let's focus on what's ahead."

Dirk took over their responses then. He insisted until they were told the whole story. A different voice addressed them from mission control then. "Are they really putting a damned appointed spokesperson on this?" Dirk asked as he shook his head. Kris only waited.

"It was the riots," the voice began, "near the labour camps. The living, they rebelled, briefly." Kris watched as Dirk grew even more agitated. "It started with a reporter. He had attended the launch. We still don't know how his article got to publication." Dirk had been against even this freedom for the living. "The article alleged a 'wild investment of both natural and capital resources' in the Hades missions. It claimed it was all a brash display of superiority. It questioned whether there was any tangible benefit to the population."

Dirk was seething when the transmission

paused. Kris could see him staring back through the floor.

"Well," the spokesperson continued, "the living were ignited overnight. It spread quickly, even to the prisoners. There was a march. The living insisted on the right to elect their own leaders again. It escalated. When it got out of hand, they targeted powerlines."

There was another pause before the spokesperson was replaced again. "It was put down. Like I said, it's under control."

"Thank…you…for informing…us," Kris responded before turning to Dirk. "Shall…we…catch up…on reports?"

Dirk worked silently as they adjusted their course to compensate for the error margins that had crept in. When they were caught up, Dirk's mood had not improved. Kris knew how deep his anger ran.

When he started to say something about the reporter, Kris insisted that the living were only misguided. "It sounds like…they reflect back…something they…themselves…would do…doesn't it?" She turned to look at Dirk. "The tribe…flaunts…its ingenuity…without seeing…its…deeper potential…without truly…committing to its future."

Dirk shook his head. "The living only see war. The news about yesterday is just one more piece of evidence." His features darkened ever further. "Perhaps we should give it to them, if they really can't see the peace we offer."

Dirk had always felt a sense of relief and justice in the fact that the labour camps provided the Hades missions with the raw manual labour they required. It was not enough. The old hatreds in him for what the living had done never truly went away, but now they flared hot. He felt something stir then—a single beat of his dead heart.

"We have been too merciful," he said, slowly.

Kris bit her lip the way she had done when she was still alive. She had made it this far without a confrontation. She was just glad that the living would inherit Earth after all this was over. Instead, she tried changing the subject. "Did you…ever want…children…before?"

Dirk didn't answer. He only tightened his hands into fists.

"I…did. I…remember…quite clearly."

If he was being honest, Dirk did too. He turned around to face Kris. It was all long ago and seemed irrelevant now. "It means nothing in the face of immortality," he said.

Several minutes passed before Kris spoke up again. "It's true…that we don't…know of anything…that can destroy us…yet. But…we may yet…find something…that does."

It could be worse, Dirk thought. The living might discover it before the dead did. He didn't answer Kris.

Their journey resumed in silence once more. Dirk watched as Kris turned her gaze outside, a hopeful glow settling on her face again. He alternated between resenting and admiring her. There was an alien and unwavering optimism in her. Nothing that had been done to her had ever dimmed it. With time, Dirk calmed down. At last, he managed to focus on what was ahead of them instead of lingering on what they had left behind.

"The Earth itself is not immortal," he said. "Where the dream will free us from a single anchor in an unforgiving universe, the living will have nowhere to flee."

Kris didn't press Dirk on what he meant by that. Then she thought of an interstellar wanderer burning its way through the atmosphere. She saw Dirk visibly relax, satisfied with what played out in his imagination. She wondered if he could hear the screaming, then resumed her work in silence.

The Hades 11 made its approach to the moon on a Saturday. The rough, pale features slowly grew into a mountainous landscape. They slipped behind their destination and into its orbit. Kris released the controls and sat back. Everything had gone according to plan. There was ground far below them once again. Dirk remarked on the geography and indicated the southern regions of the great lunar mare that was the proposed landing site. Their orbit passed in and out of the light of the sun, showing them the harsh beauty of their goal.

That Sunday, after thirty orbits around the moon, Kris and Dirk said their farewells. Her work was here aboard the command module. His was on the surface. In parting, Dirk joked that they were not to be Adam and Eve rediscovering the garden. It had made Kris rasp with laughter.

Dirk climbed into the lunar module. After all

the tests agreed with the next step of their journey, they separated. Kris inspected the exterior as their vessels drifted apart. Dirk stared back as the distance grew. He thought of the dream. He thought of Kris. He wondered whether there was something to be said for hope and joy. His gloved hands hovered over the panels as he searched for the right words. Then he decided to announce: "The *Vulture* has wings." Messages of delight answered him from Earth.

Dirk began the descent. The command module disappeared in the distance. He carried the mission now. Turning, he noted the landmarks on the surface. The moon was no more scarred than Earth had become.

"You are 'go' for landing," mission control assured him.

He was falling. By the time Dirk noticed that the craters were passing by quicker than expected, there was no keeping up with the issues as they piled up. He reported program alarm codes back to mission control as they flashed by on a screen. Not for the first time that journey, they evaded his questions.

The plummet of the lunar module did not match the simulations. He could slow himself down further, but it would burn close to his fuel reserves and he would fly right over and past the landing site. He would come down on an unknown surface, but he had no choice. The computer's newly altered trajectory would put him right in a field strewn with boulders. Mission control had yet to come back to him on the program alarms. He took manual control of the module, descending, pitching.

He was still going too fast by far. Ahead, he could see the obstacles the computer had put in his path. At this speed, he wouldn't be able to land just short of them. The next opportunity he spotted would land him in another crater. The supply of propellant was running short.

From the command module, Kris listened in silence. She could no longer see the lunar module down below. She worried for Dirk. It had become a rare thing to feel anything so strongly. She caught herself pulling on a lock of hair, another one of many nervous ticks she had acquired while alive. It tore out at the roots.

She could hear Dirk counting down the distance to the surface. She stopped herself from biting her lip. He sounded calm. She had always known that there was a chance that she wouldn't come back from this mission. She had also known that there was a chance she would have to return to Earth alone. Previous Hades missions had made it this far—into the moon's orbit. No one had ever done what Dirk was doing.

Mission control cut through. "We copy you down." Silence followed.

There was the sound of a transmission starting. Then Dirk's voice announced, "The *Vulture* has landed."

Dirk had been breathing needlessly. There was a burning pain in his lungs from years of disuse. He tried to compose himself, taking a few moments with his eyes closed. By all odds, he should have crashed, and yet he had made it. He was on the moon. The landing had been a success against all odds. The Hades missions had taken the Nation of the Dead one step closer to fulfilling the dream.

It was midnight at mission control. Dirk was surprised at how comfortable he had become with weightlessness. Everything ached when he tried to rise. Slowly, he began to prepare himself to step outside. The mission was not over. There were still things left to do. As dangerous as the landing had been, Dirk had yet to take the greatest risk.

Still adjusting to the moon's gravity, Dirk struggled to get into his suit. When he was finally able to rise, he did so awkwardly. At least he was calm once more. It was time to depressurise the lunar module and step outside.

In vacuum, Dirk forced himself through the narrow opening into a bright night sky. He clung to the narrow ladder that would take him to the moon's surface. A plaque had been attached to the exterior of the lunar module there. It read: "Here the dead of planet Earth seek peace for all their kind." Instead of the astronauts' signatures, an illustration of two small blades was engraved at the bottom.

As Dirk descended the last steps, he felt that he should say something. All he could think was that this was the farthest anyone had ever come. "This is a small step for the dead," he announced, thinking that it was not yet far enough. "Now, we will take the great leap through the darkness." He imagined mission control silenced in awe, then made his way forward, bounding away on an endless expanse of colourless rock.

"The ground's pale," he continued. "It's as fine as dust."

Dirk was about to comment on the craters and ridges when he saw that the Earth loomed ahead of him, just above the horizon. He felt something stir inside him again. He thought back to the day of the launch. He remembered looking up at the moon before dawn. Now he was looking back. A sudden beat of his heart shocked him just once more. He marvelled and turned back to see the landing site. Then he decided he should be getting to work.

Dirk retrieved the pre-packaged tools and set up a camera. Mostly, he gathered rock samples for analysis back on Earth. There was also a reflector he mounted for the purpose of further measurements of the distance to the moon, if nothing else. He described its angle. There was no response from mission control. Even after he deployed the seismic experiment, he heard only Kris' encouragement. Looking back, Dirk saw the trail of his own footsteps and found them more significant than any of the tasks he had checked off his list.

He extended a telescopic rod then. At its very end, a canvas of dark cloth unfurled. On it, an illustration of a single white skull danced back and forth as Dirk planted the flag deep into the rock. This was to become the symbol of the Nation of the Dead and their dream. Dirk stepped back from it and stared. He wondered where they would build their first colony. It would outshine all the necropoli that they had built on Earth. He felt his chest through the suit, but nothing more stirred inside of him.

One last task awaited Dirk as he returned to the lunar module. This was what he had volunteered for, despite the dangers. Dirk announced that he was starting the final experiment. He could hear Kris hesitate after starting a transmission. Mission control cut in with something unintelligible. After a long silence, Dirk sat down in view of the camera and turned to face Earth.

He took a last needless breath, then exhaled slowly. He reached up to his collar and unfastened it, gently letting all of the air escape. He felt the strain before long and closed his eyes as his corpse adjusted. Unable to speak, he waved at the camera, signalling that he had achieved vacuum. Dirk wondered how many were watching to witness what he was doing. Next, he removed his helmet and shrugged out of his spacesuit. He waved again, now completely exposed to the sun's unbridled radiation.

All was silent and would remain silent. He would have no voice and hear no sound until he rejoined Kris in orbit. He trusted that the population, both living and dead, watched his proof for all to see that they could go anywhere. He waved once more at the camera, and for the first time in years, a joyful grin showed on Dirk's face. The skin of his cheeks tore to make room for it.

Dirk wondered where they would go next. Would the dead become nomads of the void? Would they settle on a distant planet? How long before they could cut all ties with Earth?

Dirk remained still until he saw the flashing light signal on the sleeve of his suit. Protocols dictated that Kris would signal the passing of time to him along with a dozen other semaphores. Dirk found his flesh frozen in place and unresponsive to a frown. Kris was encoding a message. He waited as it was repeated, confirming what he had glanced from the first transmission. Something was wrong with mission control.

Flesh and muscle tore as Dirk reached for the actuator to encode a response. Kris answered that while the transmission signals were strong, it was all noise. They had said nothing since the landing. Mission control had not spoken a word. "Patience" was all Dirk sent in response.

They waited together, sending little more than blinks to let the other know that they were still there. Dirk found a reserve of patience in himself that he had not known in his recent bitter years, nor in his rebellious years, nor even in his years yet alive.

He refused to re-enter his spacesuit. Instead, he continued the experiment for however long he had left on the moon. His skin turned brittle before it peeled off. His flesh slowly left his bones and fell gently to join the dust. Kris and he should have been reunited by now. Dirk remained where he was. The *Vulture* could take him back in an hour, or a day, or in a month, or even a year.

He counted the days as each flowed into the next. Sometimes, he saw the command module pass by as little more than a faint light in orbit. He watched the landing site grow dark after the sun dipped below the horizon. He watched as the terrifying radiation returned, an inch above the horizon at a time. Mostly, he watched the Earth revolve before him in a cosmic play. He thought of the great speeds and distances of his own orbit around it. He knew now that no one had witnessed what they had accomplished. He feared that no one would ever again see what he saw now.

Something in him yearned to talk with Kris in more than Morse code. At every new cycle in the celestial dance before him, he considered returning to the *Vulture* if only to see her again and hear her voice again. Each time, he rededicated himself to his goal even as the exposure slowly bared his skeleton. Not even these conditions could truly destroy what death had made of him. He told himself he was merely shedding his skin. Months had passed and Dirk had yet to run out of patience. He told himself he was blessed with immortality. The camera had long since stopped recording. Mission control remained silent. They were cut off from everything they had ever known across a vast distance of space.

Before the year was done, Dirk witnessed stars appear. They were not stars in the infinite distance, but instead on the very surface of Earth. The bright lights first grew on one continent. Within the hour, they were joined on the next. Kris was signalling, but Dirk could not look away. It burned across Earth and left the surface a mottled red and grey. No place was spared.

It was something only the living would do. Losing himself in speculation, Dirk wondered how they could have retaken their seats of power. The idea that the Nation of the Dead had failed unnerved him. They had missed something. They had been too lenient. Kris would want to return to Earth. Her transmissions confirmed it when he managed to briefly tear his eyes away from the spectacle above. He told her there was nothing they could do.

Dirk remembered the first days after death. He remembered his war, his tireless revenge. He knew that if it hadn't been for the dream, he would only have stopped when there were no more of the living left alive. The dream had saved him from that fate. It had saved him from being alone on an Earth inhabited solely by the dead. Now, the dream had stranded him here.

He watched the last of the lights go out on the blasted planet. There would be nothing left. He thought of melted metal spires and wildfire wastelands. All of humanity's history would be gone, along with its future. There would be no more Hades missions. The dream ended here, with him.

It would have been New Year's Day when Dirk made his decision. Kris asked him one last time to join her back on the command module and return to Earth. She even threw back his line about becoming man and woman in the garden. Dirk searched, but he could no longer find the part of him that wanted it. He only replied that it was no paradise where they would return to and that he would only be its serpent.

The last of Dirk's flesh sloughed off that day. The last clump of atrophied organs slipped free from his ribs. Even his skeletal frame had begun to fail him. Soon, he knew he would be no more than a sentient skull, ever watchful and patient. He looked around him one last time, at the countless constellations that were never this bright before. He put the dream behind him, just as he had put his living and his dying behind him. He rested his head on a nearby ledge where he had a vantage of Earth for the years to come, just another rock bleached by the sun until it was made indistinguishable from the rest of the terrain. He told himself this fate was not a curse.

Dirk had one sunken eye left to see with. He watched when the command module left orbit. He watched an eclipse of the Earth over the sun. Finally, he watched and wondered if Kris had been right. She had carried a torch for all to see. He too began to hope, wishing for a chance to witness life again.

Dirk could see the first patches of green returning to the lands above before the blindness came.

ABOUT THE AUTHOR

PAUL WARMERDAM has only recently started submitting fiction, starting with drabbles for Black Hare Press and most recently with flash fiction for 365 Tomorrows. He lives in the Netherlands, where there's plenty of rainy hours shut indoors with a story in mind.

Bibliography

BEYOND, Black Hare Press, 2019

Genesis Initiative, 365 Tomorrows, 2020

Hades 11, Black Hare Press, 2020

MONSTERS, Black Hare Press, 2019

Oneiroboros, 365 Tomorrows, 2020

UNRAVEL, Black Hare Press, 2019

Connect

Website: kpwarmerdam.nl/fiction

ABOUT THE PUBLISHER

BLACK HARE PRESS is a small, independent publisher based in Melbourne, Australia.

Founded in 2018, our aim has always been to champion emerging authors from all around the globe and offer opportunities for them to participate in speculative fiction and horror short story anthologies.

Connect

Website: *https://www.blackharepress.com/*
Twitter: *@BlackHarePress*